TM

S U P E R M A N
R E T U R N S™
Coming Home
by Miles Lane

Superman created by Jerry Siegel and Joe Shuster.

Superman and all related names, characters and
elements are trademarks of DC Comics.
© 2006. All rights reserved.
Visit DC Comics at www.dckids.com.

First edition. Printed and manufactured in China.
All rights reserved.
ISBN: 0-696-22961-7

We welcome your comments and suggestions. Write to us at:
Meredith Books, Children's Books,
1716 Locust St., Des Moines, IA 50309-3023.
meredithbooks.com

Clark Kent was home on the Kent farm in Smallville, Kansas. He had just returned to Earth after many years away.

Clark Kent was really Superman in disguise. He had spent five years trying to find his home planet, Krypton. What he found was a dead world.

His spaceship had landed near
the Kent family farm. His mother,
Martha, helped take care of him
after his long trip.

Clark had not slept well since his return to Earth. His thoughts kept him awake, so he took a walk.

He walked down to the old barn. Clark had always liked how quiet it was inside, and the sweet smell of the hay.

As Clark stood in the barn, he thought back to when he was a boy. That was when Clark had discovered all the amazing things he could do.

One summer morning, Clark had been doing his chores when he fell through the barn roof. But he didn't land on the ground. He stopped just above it!

Clark floated above the ground. He could fly! He could really fly!

Clark ran out into the cornfield,
jumping higher and higher and higher.

After his last jump, he flew back to the ground and ran. Clark ran so fast that the stalks of corn became green blurs as he passed.

Clark couldn't believe it—he was running faster than anything he had ever seen!

As he jumped over the water tower and onto the barn roof, he stopped. He wondered what else he could do. But he did not get to think long. The roof broke apart under his feet.

Clark fell through the barn roof
and stopped just above the ground
once more.

Clark's glasses had fallen off when he fell, so he had shut his eyes. After he stopped, he slowly opened them.

There was the barn floor under him.
He had not crashed to the ground.
Clark smiled. "Wow!" he whispered.

Just then, he saw a strange handle
sticking out from the floor. Clark
lowered himself to the ground and
pulled the handle.

A door in the floor opened, revealing stairs going down under the barn. Clark slowly walked down the steps.

He saw something big covered with a sheet. He walked over and pulled the sheet away.

What he saw looked like a giant meteor, but it was hollow. It looked like something had been kept inside.

When he peered over the edge,
he saw a gleaming white crystal
nestled inside. It glowed and hummed.

Clark reached in and picked up
the white crystal. He held it in
front of him, looking at it closely.
It didn't look like anything that he
had ever seen before.

Somehow Clark knew that the crystal
was meant for him. He knew it was
time to ask his adoptive parents
some questions about where he
came from.

Coming out of his thoughts, grown-up
Clark realized the sun had come up.
He had spent most of the night lost
in thought.

Clark knew Martha would be
making breakfast by now.
He climbed out of the cellar
and headed into the house.

"Ma, I think it's time for Superman to return to Metropolis," said Clark. "I was in the barn thinking about my superpowers."

"I was gone for so long that I needed to remember who I am and why I am here. I forgot how much I can help the world," said Clark.

Martha smiled. "I know you'll always do the right thing, Clark. I even saved your costume."

Clark knew it was time to return to Metropolis, back to his friends. He stood up and smiled. "Thanks, Ma. I knew I could count on you."

Superman was back in Metropolis, ready to take on new dangers and keep the world, and those he loved, safe from harm.

At last, Superman was home!

S U P E R M A N
R E T U R N S™

AVAILABLE
WHERE QUALITY
BOOKS ARE SOLD.

**THE LAST SON
OF KRYPTON**

**EARTHQUAKE
IN METROPOLIS!**

**COMING
HOME**

I AM SUPERMAN!

BE A HERO!